Sam was going for a walk with his brother, Peter and his sister, Alice.
"Come on Sam," said Alice.
"Stop playing with that blossom."
"Blossom!" said Sam.

"Look," said Alice. "There's a coin on the path."
She picked it up.
"Can I have it?" asked Sam.
"No," said Alice. "Finders, keepers.
I'm going to buy a new teddy bear, or a
skateboard, or a tricycle, or a…"

SMALL CHANGE

Written and illustrated by
Rob Lewis

RED FOX

1 3 4 7 3 4 0

A Red Fox Book

Published by Random House Children's Books
20 Vauxhall Bridge Road, London SW1V 2SA

A division of the Random House Group
London Melbourne Sydney Auckland
Johannesburg and agencies throughout the world

First published by The Bodley Head 1991

Red Fox edition 1992

Printed and bound in Belgium by
Proost International Book Production

ISBN 0 09 997670 6

"It's only a small coin," said Peter.
"I don't think you'll be able to buy very much
with it."
"What can I buy then?" said Alice crossly.
"One small sweet," said Peter.
Alice looked very disappointed.

"You could put it in your money box and save up
for something big," said Peter.
Alice didn't like saving up.

"Can I have it?" said Sam.
"Okay," said Alice. "If you promise to be good."
"I promise," said Sam.

Sam wrapped the coin carefully in his
handkerchief and put it in his pocket.
But he kept taking it out to look at it.

He balanced the coin on his nose.
He rolled it down the hill...
and raced after it.

Then Sam met his friend Luther.
Luther had a marble.

"Let's play races," said Luther.

Sam rolled his coin, and Luther rolled his marble.
Sam's coin kept falling over
so Luther won the most times.

Luther tried to balance the marble on his nose
and Sam tried to balance his coin.

This time Luther kept falling over,
so Sam won the most times.

They buried the coin and the marble.

Then they were pirates, digging for treasure.

They came to a well.
Sam and Luther peered in.
"It looks deep," said Luther.
"I bet it's a wishing well," said Sam.
"Be careful," said Peter. "Don't fall in."

"Let's throw your coin in the well
and see how long it takes to reach the bottom,"
said Luther.
"Okay," said Sam.
He dropped the coin...
one...
two...
three...
four...
Splash!

"It's a deep well," said Luther.

"Oh dear!" said Sam.
"I haven't got my coin anymore."

"Why don't you make a wish," said Luther.

On the way home, Alice found another coin.
"Hey! That's mine!" shouted Sam.
"I wished for it."

"Remember Sam. Finders, keepers," said Alice.
"Look Sam. Watch me roll it down the hill."
But Sam wasn't listening.
He'd seen something lying on the path.

"WOW! A ten pound note!" said Peter.
"You could buy a lot with that.
You had better show mum and dad."

"Can I have it?" said Alice.
"You can have my nice shiny coin."
"Finders, keepers," said Sam.

Sam already knew what he was going to do with
his piece of paper.
"NO, SAM!" yelled Peter and Alice.

"Blossom!" said Sam.